The Flying Vampire

Rose Impey
Illustrated by Moira Kemp

Mathew Price Limited

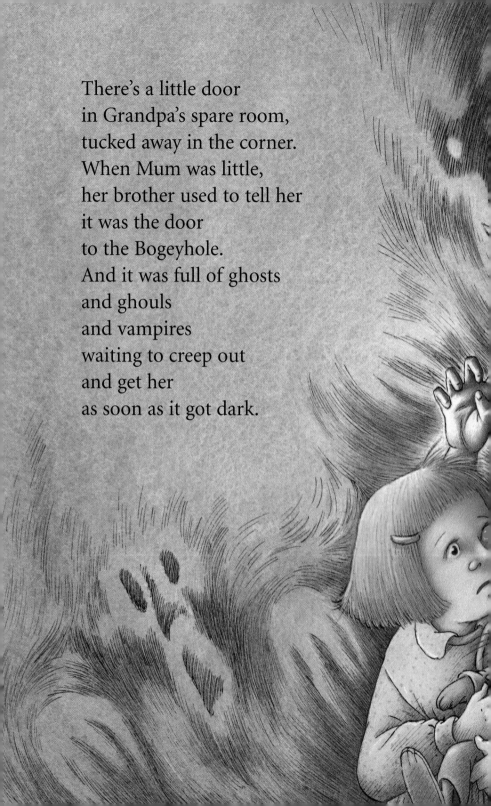

There's a little door
in Grandpa's spare room,
tucked away in the corner.
When Mum was little,
her brother used to tell her
it was the door
to the Bogeyhole.
And it was full of ghosts
and ghouls
and vampires
waiting to creep out
and get her
as soon as it got dark.

To my sister Ann
RI

To James
MK

Rose Impey has become one of Britain's most prominent children's story tellers. She used to be a primary teacher and still spends much of her time in schools reading her work to children.

Moira Kemp is a highly respected illustrator. When illustrating the 'Creepies' she drew heavily from her own childhood experience.

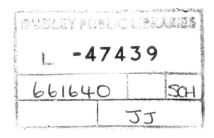
First published in 2004
by Mathew Price Ltd
The Old Glove Factory
Bristol Road, Sherborne
Dorset DT9 4HP

Designed by Douglas Martin
Produced by Mathew Price Ltd
Printed in Singapore

He was only kidding;
trying to scare her.
He's like that, my uncle Rob.
But now, when I go to stay with Grandpa,
I have to sleep in that room,
the room with the Bogeyhole.

I'm not really scared;
I know it was only a joke.
But before I get into bed
I ask Grandpa to show me,
just to be sure.
"There you are," he says.
"Just a lot of old junk.
Nothing to be afraid of."

I peer inside, but all I can see
are big dark shapes
and spooky-looking shadows.

And I wish Grandpa would
close the door, quickly,
before any of them get out.

Hidden behind the door
is a big kite shaped like a dragon.
"I'd forgotten all about this," says Grandpa.

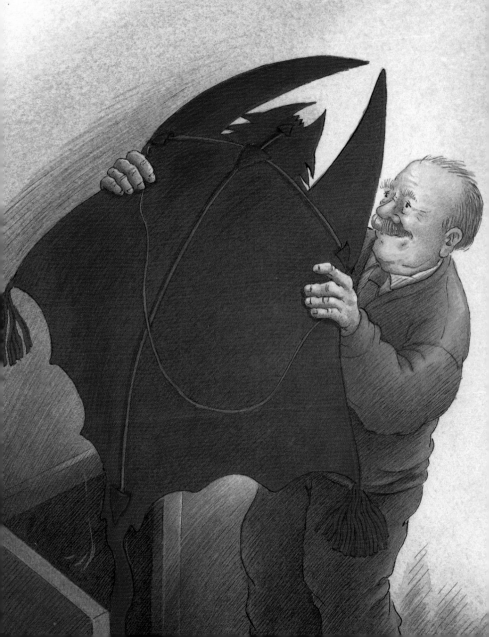

And he takes it out and hangs it
on the wall right over my bed.
"If you go straight to sleep," he says,
"we'll fly this tomorrow."

But how can I go to sleep
when I'm lying here,
on my own in the dark,
thinking about all those shapes and
shadows in the Bogeyhole?

And how can I close my eyes
when I need to keep them wide open
and fixed on that door,
just in case?

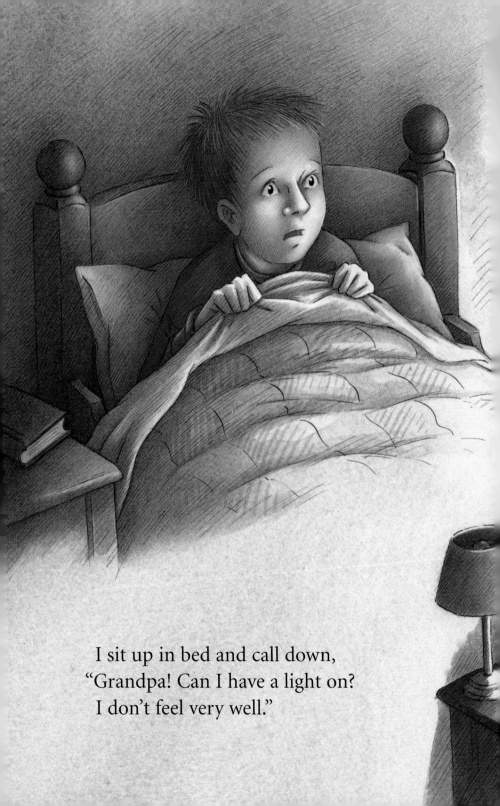

I sit up in bed and call down,
"Grandpa! Can I have a light on?
I don't feel very well."

Grandpa comes up
and finds me a nightlight.
He sits on my bed, stroking my head,
telling me jokes.

So I'm okay now.
I know there's nothing to be afraid of.
There are no such things as ghosts
and ghouls
and vampires.
It was only Uncle Rob's joke.

And I turn over onto my side
and watch the nightlight flickering,
casting shadows round the room.
Long thin spiky ones
and little soft blobby ones.

There's one that looks like a big dragon.
It's the kite Grandpa hung
on the bedroom wall.
The kite that came out of the Bogeyhole.
But now it looks like a *flying vampire*.
. . . and its starting to move.

I'm not really scared.
I know it's only the flame from the nightlight;
the hot air rising makes the kite flutter.
But it looks as if its wings
are gently rising and falling,
rising and falling,
as if it's about to take flight.

hoosh! suddenly its whole body rises up
d flaps as if it's coming to life.
try not to panic.
know it's only a kite.
ut it did come out of the Bogeyhole.
d then I start to think
rhaps it really is a Flying Vampire
ust pretending to be a kite.

I lie there holding my breath,
watching it.
But how can I watch it
and keep my eye on the door?

Because I'm starting to wonder
what else could come
creeping out of the Bogeyhole
now that my back is turned.

I roll over quickly, so I can watch the door.
But *now* I can't keep my eye on
The Flying Vampire!
Any moment it could really start to fly.

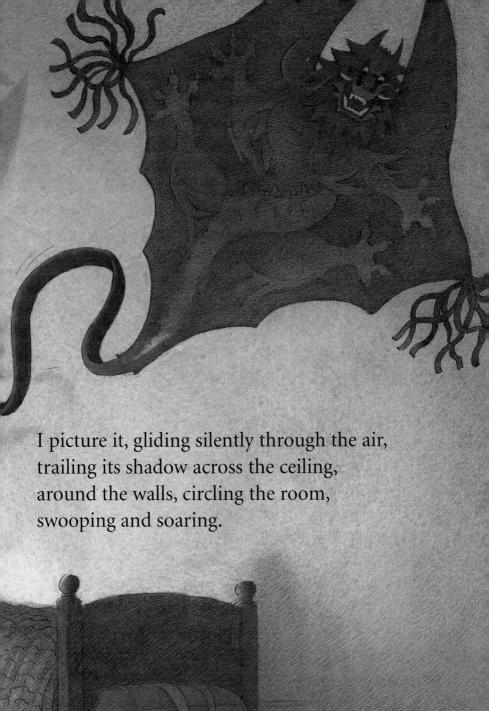

I picture it, gliding silently through the air,
trailing its shadow across the ceiling,
around the walls, circling the room,
swooping and soaring.

I can feel its sharp beady eyes
fixed on me right now;
its mouth wide open;
its fangs ready to sink into me.

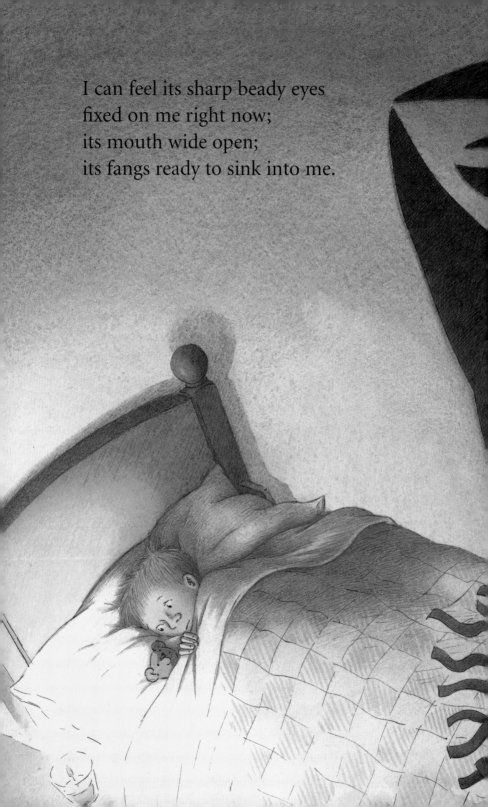

I duck down under the covers,
and pretend I'm in a tent.
I squeeze my eyes shut.
But I can still picture
The Flying Vampire
hovering over my bed,
preparing to pounce.

Here it comes! Diving Down!
Its claws stretched out;
its wings beating so fast
I can almost hear them.

But I'm ready for it.
I know what to do with vampires.
I throw off the covers
"Keep back!" I say.

Then I grab my pillow,
swinging it round and round,
beating it off.

The Flying Vampire flies up in the air.
It races across the room,
crash-landing on the carpet
right in front of the door,
the door to the Bogeyhole.

I climb out of bed,
keeping my eyes fixed on it,
and creep across the carpet.

I'm not scared now;
I know it's only a kite.
So I open the door and throw it back inside.
"Back you go," I say.
"Back to the Bogeyhole."

But I close the door with a loud SLAM!
– just in case.

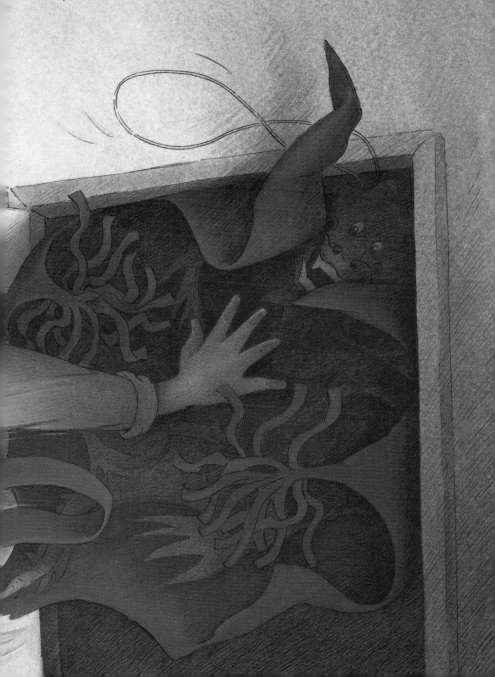